Sylvia's Spinach

by Katherine Pryor

illustrated by Anna Raff

Readers
to Eaters

Bellevue, Washington

Text copyright © 2012 by Katherine Pryor
Illustrations copyright © 2012 by Anna Raff

READERS to EATERS Books
12437 SE 26th Place, Bellevue, WA 98005
Distributed by Publishers Group West

www.ReadersToEaters.com
Follow us on Facebook and Twitter

Printed in the U.S.A. by Worzalla, Stevens Point, Wisconsin (10/12)

FSC
www.fsc.org
MIX
Paper from
responsible sources
FSC® C002589

Book design by Kate Apostolou
Book production by The Kids at Our House
The text is set in Soupbone.
The art is done in ink washes combined with pen, pencil, and other dry media,
then assembled digitally.

10 9 8 7 6 5 4 3 2 1
First Edition

Library of Congress Control Number: 2012938413
ISBN 978-0-9836615-1-1

For Todd. My favorite person to eat vegetables with is you. —K.P.

For Mom and Dad. —A.R.

Sylvia Spivens always said no to spinach.

"No spinach with my eggs! No spinach in my soup!
No spinach on my sandwich!

"No spinach! Ever!"

Sylvia's parents sighed as she pulled the spinach from her lasagna, plucked the spinach from her salad, and pushed every last leaf to the tippiest tip of her plate.

"But it's good for you," said Sylvia's mother.

"You need your growing food," said Sylvia's father.

"No, thank you!" said Sylvia.

On a drizzly gray day in March, Sylvia's teacher had an announcement:

"Class, we are going to start a garden. We'll grow peas and lettuce and carrots. We'll grow potatoes and tomatoes and squash. We'll grow cucumbers and radishes and spinach."

"Bleh!" said Sylvia.

The teacher handed each student a packet of seeds.

Wouldn't you know it? Sylvia got. . .spinach!

"Double bleh," said Sylvia.

Sylvia tried to trade for Penelope's peas.

"No way," said Penelope, rolling the little green balls in her hand.

She tried to trade for cucumbers, tomatoes, or squash.

"Nope," said Carlos.

"Forget it," said Terri.

"Sorry," said Sam.

Sylvia asked her teacher to please, please, please give her another vegetable. Any other vegetable.

"I'm sorry, Sylvia," said her teacher. "There aren't any more."

Sylvia was stuck with spinach.

Sylvia tore open the packet and looked at the little brown seeds in her hand.

Sylvia's seeds looked so. . .un-spinachy.

Sylvia followed her teacher's instructions and covered each seed with a thin layer of dirt. Then she sprinkled the seeds with water and put them in the classroom's sunniest window.

"Now what?" asked Sylvia.

"Now we wait!" said her teacher.

Days passed, and the dirt still looked like dirt.

The peas were the first to sprout, shooting up out of the dirt like tiny beanstalks.

Sylvia's dirt still looked like dirt.

The cucumbers and squash sprouted next, sending two round leaves out of each seed.

Sylvia's dirt still looked like dirt.

One by one, all of the other seeds sprouted.

"Stupid spinach," muttered Sylvia.

On the first sunny day in April, Sylvia's spinach sprouted, sending two long shoots poking out of the dirt.

The plants were smaller than Sylvia's smallest finger, but strong enough to push their way toward the sun.

"There you are!" Sylvia shouted. "My spinach!"

Every day, Sylvia checked on her baby spinach. "Good morning!" she whispered. She watered her spinach and made sure it got just exactly the right amount of sunlight. And every day, Sylvia's spinach grew a little bit taller and a little bit stronger.

On a blue-sky day in May, the students planted their garden. They planted peas and carrots and lettuce. They planted potatoes and tomatoes and squash. They planted cucumbers and radishes and. . .Sylvia planted her spinach.

Weeks passed. The sun shone. The rain rained.
And every day, Sylvia's spinach got a little bit bigger and
a little bit rounder.

The peas sent long, wavy shoots up toward the sky. The
cucumbers and squash grew big, rough leaves that even the slugs
wouldn't eat.

By the last week of school, Penelope's pea plants had beautiful white flowers, but no peas.

Terri's tomato plants had tiny yellow star flowers, but no tomatoes.

Carlos's cucumbers and Sam's squash had big yellow flowers the size of Sylvia's hand, but no cucumbers or squash.

There were only three vegetables ready to eat in the garden: lettuce, radishes, and Sylvia's spinach.

"Class, the best part about having a garden is eating what we've grown!" said Sylvia's teacher.

So the class nibbled on fresh lettuce.

They bit into fat red radishes.

And everyone munched on bright green spinach leaves.

Everyone except Sylvia.

Sylvia sniffed the spinach. It didn't smell bad.

Then Sylvia stuck out her tongue. Licked. It didn't taste bad.

Finally Sylvia opened her mouth and bit that spinach leaf in half.

Crunch!

"Not bad," said a very surprised Sylvia.

As the other students picked a little of this and a little
of that to take home to their families, Sylvia picked bunches
and bunches of spinach.

After school, Sylvia raced home to deliver her spinach.

"Look, Mom. Look, Dad," called Sylvia. "Look at my spinach!"

"It's beautiful," said her mother.

"It looks scrumptious," said her father.

"But Sylvia, what will we do with it? asked her mother. "You don't like spinach!"

"I tried it, Mom!" Sylvia said. "It's good! We can do anything we want with it."

That night, Sylvia tried spinach in
her lasagna. She nibbled spinach in her
salad. And wouldn't you know it?
Sylvia's spinach was delicious!

The next day, Sylvia ate spinach with her eggs. She ate spinach in her soup. She ate spinach on her sandwich.

And that was the summer Sylvia Spivens said yes to spinach.

Do You Want to Plant a Garden?

Plants need a few basic things to survive and thrive: sun, soil, and water. Different plants like different amounts of sun and water. A tomato plant likes a lot of sun and warmth, while a leafy green such as spinach can handle cooler weather and a bit of shade. If the leaves start to droop, the plant is probably thirsty and wants a drink of water.

Soil—a fancy word for good dirt—is where the plant gets the food it needs to grow. Plants—like humans—need certain nutrients to grow big and strong. Making sure you have healthy soil is the best way to grow healthy plants!

You can grow a garden in many ways. If you're planting a garden directly in the dirt, make sure an adult gets the soil tested for toxins, such as lead, that may have been left behind. Another great way to garden is in raised beds—just build a four-sided wooden box on top of the ground and fill it with good soil. You can also grow food in big pots on a sunny balcony or patio if you don't have much space.

What do you want to plant? It's good to plant foods you like to eat, but you have to make sure the plant can grow in the climate where you live. Plants such as melons and chili peppers need hot weather and a lot of sun. Plants such as peas and broccoli do well in cooler places.

Most people plant their gardens in the spring and harvest food in the summer and fall. It's a good idea to plant things that will ripen at different times to make sure you can eat fresh food for a whole season.

The most important part of having a garden? Having fun! Don't be afraid to experiment and try something new, just like Sylvia.

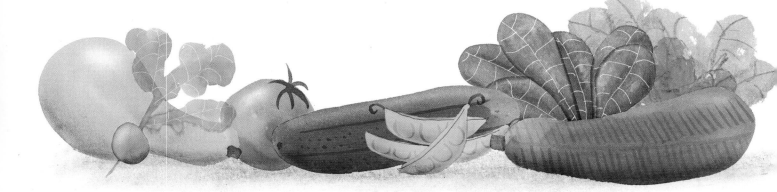